ScaredyBat

and the Missing Jellyfish

By Marina J. Bowman

Illustrated by Yevheniia Lisovaya

Code Pineapple

This is a work of fiction. Names, characters, places, and incidents either are the product of the author's imagination or are used fictitiously. Any resemblance to actual persons, living or dead, events, or locales is entirely coincidental.

First paperback edition August 2020

Written by Marina J. Bowman
Illustrated by Yevheniia Lisovaya
Book Design by Lisa Vega

ISBN 978-1-950341-16-0 (paperback black & white)
ISBN 978-1-950341-17-7 (paperback color)
ISBN 978-1-950341-15-3 (ebook)

Published by Code Pineapple
www.codepineapple.com

For all who fear the deep, dark unknown,
but dive in anyway because some of the best
things in life are found there.

Also by Marina J. Bowman

SCAREDY BAT

A supernatural detective series for kids with courage, teamwork, and problem solving. If you like solving mysteries and overcoming fears, you'll love this enchanting tale!

#1 Scaredy Bat and the Frozen Vampires

#2 Scaredy Bat and the Sunscreen Snatcher

#3 Scaredy Bat and the Missing Jellyfish

THE LEGEND OF PINEAPPLE COVE

A fantasy-adventure series for kids with bravery, kindness, and friendship. If you like reimagined mythology and animal sidekicks, you'll love this legendary story!

#1 Poseidon's Storm Blaster

#2 A Mermaid's Promise

Free Jellyfish Lake Coloring Pages

As a gift, we'd like to give you FREE Jellyfish Lake coloring pages so you can unleash your creativity and add your own color to the story!

GO HERE TO GET YOUR COLORING PAGES NOW:

scaredybat.com/book3bonus

Detective Team

Ellie

aka Scaredy Bat “the detective”

Jessica
"the courage"

Fez

“the heart”

Tink
"the brains"

Contents

Batty Bonuses

Can you solve the mystery?

All you need is an eye for detail, a sharp memory, and good logical skills. Join Ellie on her mystery-solving adventure by making a suspect list and figuring out who committed the crime! To help with your sleuthing, you'll find a suspect list template and hidden details observation sheets at the back of the book.

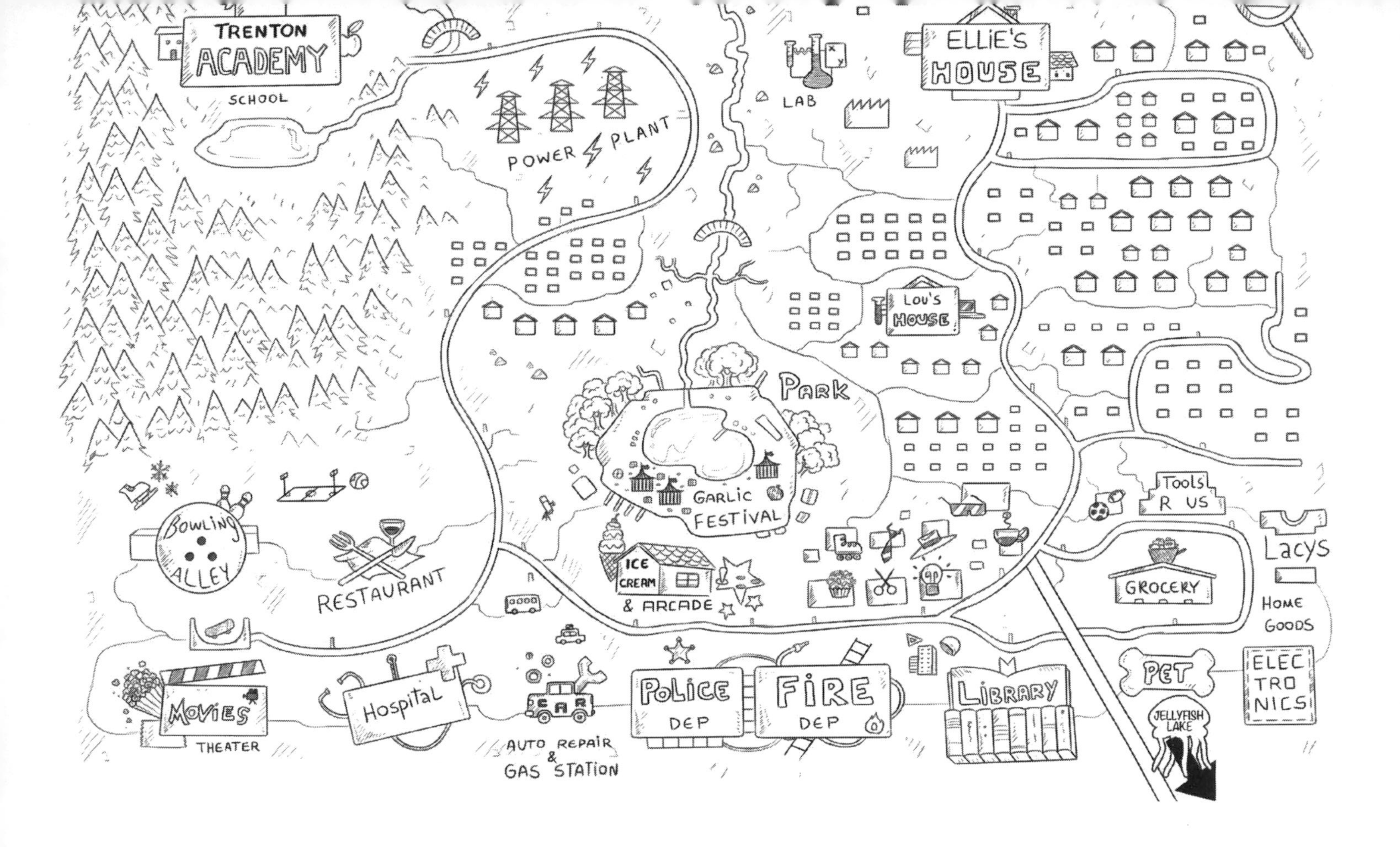
TRENTON ACADEMY
SCHOOL
POWER PLANT
LAB
ELLIE'S HOUSE
LOU'S HOUSE
PARK
GARLIC FESTIVAL
BOWLING ALLEY
RESTAURANT
ICE CREAM & ARCADE
TOOLS R US
LACYS
HOME GOODS
GROCERY
CAR
MOVIES
THEATER
HOSPITAL
AUTO REPAIR & GAS STATION
POLICE DEP
FIRE DEP
LIBRARY
PET
JELLYFISH LAKE
ELEC TRO NICS

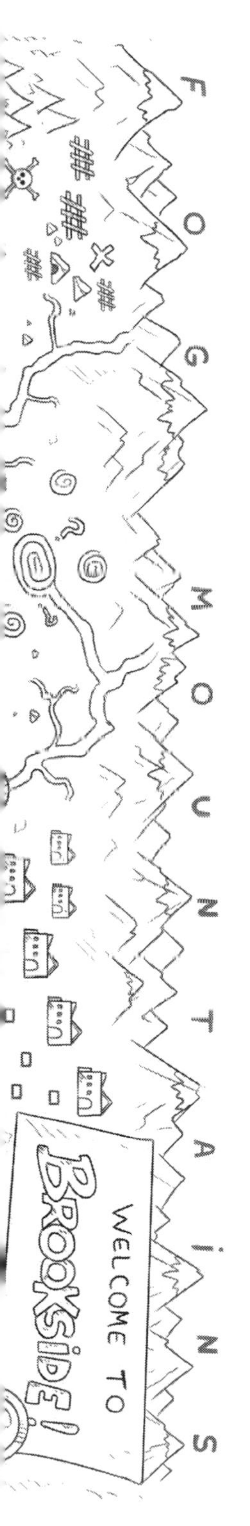

There's a place not far from here
With strange things 'round each corner
It's a town where vampires walk the streets
And unlikely friendships bloom

When there's a mystery to solve
Ellie Spark is the vampire to call
Unless she's scared away like a cat
Poof! There goes that Scaredy Bat

Villains and pesky sisters beware
No spider, clown, or loud noise
Will stop Ellie and her team
From solving crime, one fear at a time

Chapter One

A Jerky Bus Ride

TUNK!

The school bus hit a large bump, spilling the contents of Ellie's pink backpack across the aisle. With a groan, Ellie scooped up her pajamas, bathing suit, detective notepad, and some snacks—everything she needed for the overnight class trip to Jellyfish Lake. She stuffed it all back into her bag, but something very important was missing.

"My sunscreen!" Ellie said with a gasp. "No, no, no. This can't be happening again." She leaned down to look under the seat, but all she found was a dust bunny and wads of chewed bubble gum.

"Found it!" came a cheerful voice. Ellie

flipped back up to face the round, smiling face of one of her best friends, Fez. He extended the sunscreen toward Ellie across the aisle.

With a sigh of relief, she grabbed it and gently placed it into her backpack. "Thank you!" Ellie said, but Fez's attention was now somewhere else. In his other hand, he held a stick of wrinkled meat sheathed in plastic.

"Jelly Belly Liver Jam Jerky," he read off the label. "If it doesn't make you feel perky, it isn't Jelly Belly Jerky." Fez's eyes grew wide with excitement. "Well, that's one delicious tongue twister," he exclaimed, licking his lips.

"Go ahead," said Ellie, stifling a small giggle. She'd never expected someone to look so jazzed about jam jerky. But she supposed if anyone were going to be excited about jelly-filled meat, it would be Fez. He eagerly tore into the package and took a big bite out of the meat stick. A stream of green jelly promptly squirted out, giving the bat design on his t-shirt a goopy beard. But Fez didn't seem to notice.

"This is soooo good," he exclaimed. "It's salty, tangy, and..." He licked his lips. "Just a little bit sweet. How have I never had this before!?"

"I think only the vampire grocery stores have it," explained Ellie. "And it's pretty new. I haven't even tried it yet."

Fez popped the last piece of gooey meat into his mouth just as she spoke.

"Oops." He held up the empty wrapper and gave a big swallow. "Sorry."

Ellie laughed. "That's okay. I have more! They're also coming out with a glowing jelly next month! I can't wait to make a glowing bone marrow butter and jelly sandwich." Ellie's mouth watered at the thought. She dug in her backpack for another meat stick just as Jessica walked to the back of the bus.

Jessica's red curls bounced as she plopped down beside Ellie and exhaled dramatically. "Please tell me you haven't lost your sunscreen again," Jessica said with an eye roll as she watched Ellie shuffle around the contents of her backpack. "I do not want to waste our field trip to Jellyfish Lake looking for sunscreen. Or hearing you complain about turning blue from the sun."

Before Ellie could even respond to her oldest friend's curiously catty comment, Fez chimed in from across the aisle. "I still think it's so odd that you vampires can permanently turn blue from too much sun, or even lose your transformational powers. Crazy."

"No, what's really crazy is how long this drive is taking," Jessica complained. "We've been on this bus forever."

"Why are you so crabby?" Ellie asked.

Jessica wrinkled her nose. "Gah. I'm not. This is just the longest bus ride ever. I want to get off of this hot sticky bus and swim."

"Me, too!" agreed Fez. "I think I want to write my report about swimming with jellyfish. It was one of the ideas on the handout."

Fez smoothed out a crumpled sheet he pulled from his pocket.

Grade 7 – Jellyfish Lake Report

Ideas to get you started:

1. *Your personal experience swimming in Jellyfish Lake. It should be unique, since this is one of the only lakes in the world where you can swim with jellyfish.*
2. *Tourism and how it supports the Jellyfish Lake Science Camp and preservation of the lake.*
3. *The lake's history. These beaches are where the Fang and Flesh Treaty was first signed. Vampires and humans lived in harmony here long before it became more widespread.*
4. *The ecosystem and animals surrounding the lake.*
5. *Of course, you are welcome to use your own ideas, but these should get those brain juices flowing.*

Happy swimming!

Ellie got to the last line, and her breath caught in her throat.

"I am *not* going swimming," she declared.

"Why not!?" asked Fez. "The best part about Jellyfish Lake is you can swim with the jellyfish."

Ellie looked around the bus at all the other kids, who were enthusiastically chatting away. She leaned over Jessica toward Fez and lowered her voice to a whisper.

"I'm scared of swimming in lakes."

"What?" Fez asked.

Ellie cleared her throat and said it slightly louder, her cheeks getting warm. "I'm scared of swimming in lakes."

"What? I can't hear you," said Fez.

"Oh, for the love of pudding!" erupted Jessica. "She said she is scared of swimming in lakes!" She lowered her voice to a mutter. "She's called Scaredy Bat for a reason."

The kids in neighboring seats turned to look at the commotion. Ellie's face burned hot, and she sank down in the seat to avoid their gazes. The back of the blue bus seat may have been able to shield her from their judging looks, but it couldn't protect her from their giggles and whispers. Ellie clapped her hands over her ears.

SCREEEECH! Ellie jerked forward as the bus came to a hard stop. The squeal of the bus's brakes pierced through her makeshift hand earmuffs.

"Did you see that!?" bellowed the bus driver. "There was a monster! A big brown furry one, right in the middle of the road."

Chapter Two

The Wonders of Jellyfish Lake

Everyone stood to try to catch a glimpse of the monster. Out of the corner of her eye, Ellie spotted a large, rustling bush through the smudged bus window. But when she turned for a better look, the bush was still. *Could there really be a monster*? she wondered.

As if reading Ellie's thoughts, Mr. Bramble's deep voice boomed over the commotion. "Sit down, everyone. Sit down," he urged in the same loud voice he used when teaching. "There is nothing to see. It was probably just a bear—certainly not a monster." Mr. Bramble turned toward the bus driver and gave a deep sigh, clearly unimpressed that he had caused such a fright.

The bus driver, who had big round glasses that made his eyes look like an owl's, only gave a slight shrug. "But I could have sworn I saw—"

"Please return to your seats so we can get on our way," Mr. Bramble interrupted. "We should only be about ten minutes out from the camp now."

Ellie's heart thumped hard against the wall of her chest as she slid back down in her seat and propped her knees up. Her embarrassment was quickly overtaken by thoughts of what the bus driver saw. What if there really was a monster? Or was Mr. Bramble right, and it was just a bear? Ellie knew exactly who to ask. She scooted past Jessica and walked to the front of the bus. Right in the front seat was a boy with curly brown hair and glasses. He had his face buried in a large book.

"Hey, Tink," Ellie said, sitting in the seat behind him. "Why are you all the way up here?"

Tink lifted his face out of the book and smiled.

"Oh, hey, Ellie. I just wanted some quiet to read." He turned his book cover toward her and pointed to the title: *The Wonders of Jellyfish Lake*. "Have you read this?" he asked. "It's absolutely fascinating." Before Ellie could answer, Tink continued, "For example, did you know that jellyfish have no eyes, bones, brains, or hearts? They are made mostly of water. And the type of jellyfish found in Jellyfish Lake don't sting, which is why it's such a popular tourist attraction. And freshwater jellyfish are in danger due to pollution. And jellyfish have— "

Ellie interrupted, knowing that Tink could go on all day about the facts he'd learned. "Does that book say anything about"—Ellie lowered her voice to a whisper—"any brown and furry monsters?"

Tink adjusted his glasses on his nose and thumbed through a few pages.

"Hmm, so far it hasn't, but I'm only about halfway through."

Ellie nibbled on her nails. Tink offered her a smile and lowered his voice. "You know, what the bus driver saw was probably just a bear, or even a moose. And have you seen the size of his glasses? I don't know how he drives, let alone identifies a monster."

Ellie looked up at the bus driver, who had earphones stuffed in his ears. His glasses really were thick. She watched as a fly landed on his nose, and he smacked himself in the face. The fly buzzed away and landed on Ellie's turquoise trench coat. Ellie and Tink both snickered.

"Thanks, Tink," Ellie said, sighing with relief.

Mr. Bramble got to his feet a few seats away and hushed the class.

"If I can have everyone's attention, I have a little surprise. By now, you all know about the presentation and report you have to do on Jellyfish Lake. The fact that it's worth thirty percent of your grade should be enough incentive to do your best work. But as a bonus, there will be a prize for the top three projects."

Everyone on the bus started whispering about what it could be. Ellie's classmates guessed everything from a new bike to a pass for the new amusement park.

Mr. Bramble hushed the class once again. "The three best projects will get to go to Jellyfish Lake!" The class became silent.

"Isn't that where we're going?" asked a girl with two green braids.

"Right you are," said Mr. Bramble. "But the winners will get a spot at Jellyfish Lake's Science Camp this year, with special guest counselor Bonnie Samson." The class remained silent, but Mr. Bramble didn't seem to notice

the lack of enthusiasm. “So you better start thinking about those projects!”

Ellie groaned. “I should have known any surprise by Mr. Bramble would be lame,” she whispered to Tink.

“Lame!?” Tink said in genuine shock. “Bonnie Samson is anything but lame. She is absolutely amazing.”

“Who is that?” Ellie asked.

"You don't know who Bonnie Samson is!?"

Ellie shrugged.

"She is an amazing scientist. She figured out how to isolate the invisibility gene in ghosts and is running tests on how to apply it to different species."

"That's pretty neat," Ellie said genuinely, but apparently not with enough excitement to satisfy Tink.

"Pretty neat? Let me put it this way," Tink tried again. "I feel about Bonnie Samson how you feel about Hailey Haddie." Now *that* Ellie fully understood. She didn't know what she would do if she ever got to meet her hero, actress Hailey Haddie. AKA the best vampire detective ever.

"Wow, you must really like her!" Ellie concluded. "I wish there was a way I could meet Hailey Haddie."

Tink nodded enthusiastically. "Like I said, AMAZING. Now, I really have to finish this book."

"Okay. Well, come sit with us if you get sick of reading."

Tink laughed. "I don't think I could ever get sick of reading!" Tink lifted his book back up to his face. "Especially not this chapter; it talks about how there are half a million jellyfish in Jellyfish Lake."

"That's a lot! Are there really that many?" Ellie asked.

Tink was now fully immersed in his book and didn't hear Ellie.

Mr. Bramble cleared his throat as Ellie stood. "Actually, there aren't quite that many jellyfish anymore," he explained. "In fact, I got an email this morning saying that many seem to be going missing lately."

"Oh, where do you think they're going?" Ellie asked.

Mr. Bramble furrowed his brow. "Not sure. It's a real mystery."

Ellie let out a large gasp, and her eyes widened. If this was a mystery, then she was on the case!

Chapter Three

I Spy With My Little Eye

Ellie pranced back to her seat as Jessica scooted to the spot closest to the window. Ellie would tell her friends about the case later, but first, she wanted to find a lead.

"Ooo! Wanna play I Spy?" asked Fez as soon as he spotted Ellie. "I'm great at this game." Without waiting for Ellie to sit, or even agree, Fez began. "I spy with my little eye something that is brown."

Jessica sat in silence as Ellie played along while she dug for her notebook. She guessed everything from Jessica's sweater to the gunk stuck on the bus's windowsill. But after several minutes, she still couldn't figure it out.

"I give up," Ellie said eventually as her

stomach gave a monstrous growl. "I'm too hungry and distracted. What is it?" She reached in her backpack and searched for a stick of jerky.

"It's the mark on Jessica's arm! It kind of looks like a mouse," said Fez with a big grin.

But when Ellie turned to see what he was talking about, Jessica had already tugged the

leopard-print sleeve down to hide the brown spot. She sprang to her feet and looked at Ellie, who had finally found the Jelly Belly Liver Jam Jerky.

"If you're going to eat that disgusting thing, I'm going to sit somewhere else," Jessica scoffed. She paused for a second to stifle a sneeze before climbing over Ellie and making her way to an empty seat a few rows back. Ellie and Fez shared a confused glance. Jessica was never afraid to speak her mind, but she wasn't normally mean about it—especially not to her best friend, Ellie.

"It definitely seems like something is bugging Jessica," said Fez as Ellie turned to look at Jessica, who was staring out the window in her new seat.

"Definitely," Ellie agreed. It was odd that she was so crabby. And why would she be wearing a sweater on the bus when she said she was hot earlier? Ellie's stomach growled once again, interrupting her thoughts. Ellie gave her mopey-looking friend one last glance before turning her attention to her notebook.

After a few minutes of scribbling, though, she hadn't gotten very far—she'd only managed to doodle a jellyfish and a blank numbered list of clues and suspects.

Ellie's stomach grumbled once more. *Maybe I just need some food*, she thought. She finally peeled open the stick of jerky, but before she could take a bite, it was gone.

SCREEEECH! The jerky flew out of her hand as the bus once again came to a sudden stop.

Not another monster, Ellie thought.

"Oops," said the bus driver. "Hit the brakes a bit too hard that time. Sorry! But we're here."

Fez pointed to the Jam Jerky on the ground. "Are you going to eat that?"

Ellie looked at a dust bunny near her snack and slumped her shoulders.

"No. Go ahead."

Fez scooped it off the ground and gave it a good blow before chomping down.

Everyone slowly poured out of the bus onto the pink-and-white gravel pathway that forked off to the cabins, beach, and trails. Ellie fanned

her face as the hot sun beat down. She grabbed her sunscreen and slathered it on, but soon her hands became too slippery. The bottle popped right out of her grip and rolled under the bus to the other side. Ellie walked around the bus but paused to watch a stout man and a woman in deep conversation. They both wore beige and green park ranger outfits.

"The jellyfish are just vanishing," said the plump park ranger. "If this continues, we're going to have to close the park—possibly for good."

"That's terrible," said the slender woman. "Why would we have to close the park?"

"We need to preserve the jellyfish that are left," the plump ranger explained. "With them disappearing, the whole lake's ecosystem is in danger."

"Where do you think all the jellyfish are going?"

"No idea. But between the disappearing jellyfish and those strange footprints on the beach last week, this place sure is weird lately."

"Yes!" Ellie cheered, far louder than intended. This was the lead she needed.

The two park rangers turned toward her.

"Oh, um. I…" Ellie spotted her sunscreen on the gravel near her feet. "My sunscreen!" she pointed at it. "I wasn't sure where it went, but I found it. Yippee." Ellie quickly scooped up her sunscreen and raced to tell her friends about their new case.

Chapter Four

Jinx!

When Ellie got to the other side of the bus, the class was already walking to the cabins. She ran up the line and soon found Fez and Tink. "Psst. Guys, you will never guess what." Ellie explained to them what she had just heard and how they had a mystery on their hands.

A loud snort sounded behind her just as she finished her explanation. Ellie turned around to face her least favorite person ever, Jack Grinko. A new kid this year who seemed to love making people miserable, especially Ellie and her friends.

"Look at the little Scaredy Bat making up stories. It's cute that you and your wittle friends

still play make-belief." Jack laughed.

Ellie put her hands on her hips. "I am not making this up. And I wasn't even talking to you."

Mr. Bramble clapped his hands from the front of the line, which had now come to a stop. "Miss Spark!" he shouted. "If you were listening at all, which clearly you were not, you would know that this is the line for the boy's cabin. Are you a boy?" Ellie took a good look at the line of boys. She shook her head. Mr. Bramble pointed to another line a few cabins

down. “Then that is where you need to be.”

Ellie mumbled an apology before sprinting to her lineup. She looked up and down it for Jessica, but she was nowhere in sight.

Half an hour later, after unpacking and getting into her yellow-and-blue-striped swimsuit, Ellie found herself squidging the soft, warm sand between her toes. She took in the sight of the clear turquoise lake lined with trees and cabins. She got just close enough to the lake so that the gentle waves and cool water could lick her toes—but that was as far as she would

go. She took in a deep breath, and the earthy smell of pine tickled her nostrils.

"ACHOO!" Ellie let out a big sneeze, followed by another. "ACHOO!"

"Sanalamia!" said a cheerful voice from behind Ellie. Ellie turned toward her classmate, Ava Grinko, lying on a beach chair in her purple ruffled swimsuit and oversized sunglasses. Ellie looked down at her old swimsuit and felt frumpy in comparison.

"Thanks!" said Ellie.

"You're welcome. If you're going to go for a swim, I would be happy to watch your necklace so you don't lose it," Ava offered with a big, fangy smile.

"No thanks," Ellie replied as she thumbed the purple dragon necklace that hung around her neck. A soft, cool wave washed over her foot, and she backed away. "I don't really like swimming in lakes," she added.

"Ah, me neither. It always tangles my hair," Ava said as she twirled one of her shiny black ringlets. "Let me know if you change your mind!"

Ellie smiled and nodded. "I will. Thanks!"

Ellie watched Tink and Fez in the lake. They'd decided that the two boys should go see exactly how many jellyfish there were firsthand and look for any clues. However, right now, it sure seemed like they were playing more than anything. They splashed each other, and Ellie wished she could join them. She had so much fun playing with them in the pool during the summer, but pools were safe. She knew how deep the pool was and that no monsters were lurking in the depths. The lake, on the other hand… well, anything could be in there.

Turning her attention back to the mystery, Ellie scanned the beach for any hint of mysterious creatures. But all she found were some neat rocks, a broken sandcastle shovel, a few chip bags, and some plastic bottles.

Where could the jellyfish be going? she thought. Ellie remembered what the bus driver had seen and what the park rangers said. *What if there was a lake monster, and what if he was also able to walk on the land?* However, she hadn't found

any strange footprints herself, so who knew what the ranger had seen. She wandered further down the beach.

SPLAT!

Ellie's sandal was pulled down by an orange sticky mess beside a soda can.

"Ew!" Ellie cried.

Fez and Tink emerged from the lake just in time to watch Ellie try to free her sandal from the sticky spot.

Tink scrunched up his face. "What did you step in?"

Ellie tried to wipe the orange gunk off, but her sandal just picked up more sand. She pointed to the soda can.

"Orange soda that has been cooking in the hot sun," she said.

"Ewww," said Fez and Tink at the same time.

"Jinx!" exclaimed Fez. "You owe me a..." He looked at the sticky, gross mess on the ground. "Well, maybe not a soda."

"I can't stand people who litter," said Tink. "Don't they know it pollutes the lake?"

"That's it!" exclaimed Ellie. "Tink, you're a genius. I have a new lead for the case!"

"I am pretty smart, but what did I say?" asked Tink.

But Ellie was already rushing to the lake.

Chapter Five

RIP Mr. Frog

Tink and Fez followed Ellie to the lake.

"Look at all the garbage," Ellie said. She pointed at bottles and cans littering the beach, along with aluminum wrappers and plastic packaging. "Earlier, you told me that jellyfish are in danger due to pollution, so isn't it possible that there are fewer jellyfish because the lake is polluted?"

"Yes, that is possible," agreed Tink.

"Look!" Ellie pointed to a frog that was belly-up on the shore.

"I'm going to go get my water testing kit from my backpack," Tink said. "That should help us figure out if pollution is causing this."

Soon Tink rushed back with a plastic

briefcase. He popped open the latches and pulled out a thin, white strip of paper.

"What does that do?" Fez asked.

"It will tell us the pH of the water," Tink responded. Ellie and Fez gave him a blank look. "It will tell us if the lake is too acidic or not acidic enough. Both can hurt fish. I made these test strips out of red cabbage juice and coffee filters, so they aren't as accurate as real pH strips, but they should give us an idea." Tink dipped the test strip into the lake water, and it turned a medium green.

"What does that mean?" asked Fez.

Tink pulled out a chart with a color scale that ranged from red to purple. It was also numbered 1 to 14. He held the test strip up to match the color.

"Looks like a seven," said Ellie. "Is that okay?"

"That is perfect. It means the water is neutral. If it were pink-ish red, it would mean it was acidic like a lemon. If it had turned purple-ish, then it would have been non-acidic, also known as a base, like soapy water."

"That's really neat!" Ellie exclaimed. "So you can figure out if the lake is polluted just by testing the pH of the water?"

"Not quite," answered Tink. "I wish it was that simple. PH is only one part of lake health, but besides the litter, the lake looks healthy. I was actually reading in my book today that Jellyfish Lake has some of the cleanest water in this region."

Fez turned to the frog. "What do you think happened to this guy, then?"

Tink shrugged. "Could have been too hot for him, maybe he got wounded, or maybe it was just his time."

"Poor little guy," said Fez. Fez plucked a yellow flower from a grassy patch and laid it down on the frog. "Rest in peace, Mr. Frog."

RIBBIT! The frog rolled over onto his feet and hopped toward the tall grass.

"Or I guess he could just be sleeping," said Tink.

They all laughed.

"Well, it doesn't look like pollution is to blame," Ellie said. "Did you guys see anything weird while you were swimming?"

Tink scratched his chin. "Now that I think about it, I only saw jellyfish here and there. It wasn't full of jellyfish like my book shows. In fact, there wasn't a smack anywhere."

Fez's eyes lit up. "Woah, a snack? There was supposed to be a snack?"

Tink snickered. "No, Fez. A *smack*. It's what you call a group of jellyfish."

"They should make a jelly candy called a smack snack!" declared Fez. "I would totally eat it."

"Fez, what wouldn't you eat?" Tink asked.

"Jellyfish, or frogs, or green apples."

Ellie cleared her throat. "Back to the mystery. So, there are definitely fewer jellyfish."

"Yes," Tink confirmed.

"Hey, have you seen Jessica?" Fez asked Ellie as he glanced down the beach. "I haven't seen her since we got here."

Ellie shook her head. "She eventually showed up in the girls' cabin earlier, but she was ignoring me for the most part."

A piercing scream echoed over the lake. All three of the friends looked at each other.

"Jessica!?"

They turned around, expecting to see their friend. But it was Ava standing on her beach chair. They rushed over to see what the commotion was about.

"What's going on?" asked Mr. Bramble. "Are you okay?"

Ava let out a small whimper. "I am not okay!"

“Are you hurt?” asked Mr. Bramble.

“Worse,” said Ava. “There’s a rat! A big furry rat that just ran across the beach.”

Ellie turned a ghostly white.

“That’s all?” Mr. Bramble asked. “I thought it was--”

The brown rat scurried across Ellie’s foot, and she shrieked. With a dash and a hop, she joined Ava on the chair.

Mr. Bramble ran his hand over his face. "Miss Grinko, I realize you are used to your cushy city life that is free of pests. But please, try to calm down. Screaming at the top of your lungs is uncalled for. And that also goes for you, Miss Spark," he added, looking at Ellie. "The campfire is in ten minutes, so go to your cabin and start getting ready." With an exasperated sigh, Mr. Bramble walked away, and many of the curious onlookers followed.

Ellie and Ava hopped off their chairs and looked around.

"Do you think it's gone?" Ava asked.

"Yeah, I saw it run up the hill toward the cabins," said Ellie.

"Looks like Scaredy Bat is starting to rub off on you," Jack called from across the beach.

"Jack!" Ava shrieked. "Don't you have anything better to do?"

Jack repeated what his sister had said in a mocking voice before taking off to his cabin.

Tink rolled his eyes. "I should turn him blue again." A week before Jack had snatched a lollipop from him that turned him blue.

Ava giggled. "This time, you should try purple! I think that would look great on him."

Tink looked at the ground and lowered his voice. "Oh, umm..." He used his foot to trace lines in the sand. "Yeah, that would look good on him."

Ellie looked at the sand and spotted a wrapper for Jelly Belly Liver Jam Jerky. Her stomach rumbled. She couldn't wait for campfire marshmallows. She picked up the wrapper and walked to the garbage can. Almost all of the trash in the can was Jelly Belly brand. Soda cans, chip bags, plastic bottles—they were all from Jelly Belly.

Chapter Six

Tale of the Hairy Toe

Ellie was delighted to find Jessica in bed back at the cabin. Ellie wanted to fill her in on the case of the missing jellyfish, including the newest discovery of how all the beach garbage was from the same food company. It could be a clue.

"Where have you been?" Ellie asked.

"Around," Jessica replied.

"Around where?"

"We are miles away from anywhere fun, so obviously around here," snapped Jessica.

"Jess, I know you've been excited for this trip. You even said on the bus you wanted to swim, but I didn't see you at the beach. Where

have you been? And why are you suddenly being so crabby?"

"I'm not being crabby!"

"Then you might want to know we have a new mystery," Ellie said. "And you missed looking for clues and testing the water for pollution."

"Not everything is about mysteries, Ellie."

Before Ellie could respond, the rest of the girls in her class came in to change for the campfire. Ellie pulled on her clothes, including her turquoise trench coat for extra warmth.

"Want to walk with me to the campfire?" Ellie asked Jessica.

"I don't feel well right now. I'll catch up later," Jessica answered.

"Is it your allergies? The pine smell makes me sneeze, too. Is there anything I can do?"

Jessica pulled the fleece blanket over her head. "Just leave me alone."

"Okay," said Ellie as she tried to fight back tears. "I hope you feel better soon… Love you lots." Ellie left the cabin with Ava in tow.

"You think she will be okay?" Ava asked.

"I hope so," said Ellie, wiping a tear off her cheek. "I've known her since I was four, and I've seen her sick in the past. But she was never mean about it." What could possibly be going on with Jessica? Would she ever have her best friend back?

The sweet smell of melted marshmallows filled the air around the campfire. The entire class sat on wooden benches by the fire while chatting and roasting hotdogs, veggie dogs, and marshmallows. Ellie was excited to finally get some food, since she had been hungry since the bus. She wiped a glob of ketchup off the end of her hotdog before digging in. Tink, however, was far more interested in the wonders of nature and hadn't even touched his veggie dog.

Tink pointed to the dark sky, blanketed in millions of glowing stars. "Look, there's the Big Dipper! And there's the Little Dipper," he said.

"Wow, this is way prettier than the stars at home," said Fez, putting another marshmallow on his stick.

“Much less light pollution,” Tink explained.

Ellie shoved the last of her hotdog in her mouth as she flipped open her detective note-pad. She scribbled a list by the warm glow of the fire.

Possible clues:

1. *The monster or bear the bus driver saw - maybe bears eat jellyfish?*

2. *The footprints the park ranger was talking about – didn't find any myself.*
3. *Garbage by the lake - all Jelly Belly?*

Suspects:

1. *Pollution – kills many animals, and there is garbage around the lake*
2. *Jack – he's such a bully. Maybe he bullied the jellyfish away!*
3. *Someone who needs the jellyfish for something… but who?*

She tapped her pencil on her notepad and rethought her suspect list.

1. *~~Pollution~~ – (The water tested fine and the frog wasn't dead.)*
2. *~~Jack~~ – (The jellyfish went missing before he arrived. But he's still a big bully!)*
3. *Someone who needs the jellyfish for something… but who?*

Ellie nibbled on her lip while she pondered what possible connection this could all have to the disappearing jellyfish. Who would need jellyfish and why? Maybe an aquarium ran out? Or perhaps they were worth a lot of money?

Mr. Bramble soon interrupted her thoughts. "Attention, everyone. I just got some bad news that you all need to hear. Unfortunately, Jellyfish Lake will be closing after this weekend, so the Science Camp is no longer available as a prize. So sorry to let you down. The park has decided that with all the jellyfish disappearing, it is best to protect those that are left."

He paused to let the class react, but no one seemed to care much—no one but Tink. Tink's mouth hung open as he stared at the fire.

"However, I think it is only fair that there is still a prize," Mr. Bramble continued. "So, the winner will now be getting tickets to the opening of the new theme park, Mega Adventure Land."

Everyone in the class started chatting excitedly about the new theme park and how they really wanted the tickets.

"Are you okay?" Fez asked Tink.

After a few seconds, Tink finally answered. "That Science Camp was my dream. My foster mom Shayla tried to get me in last year, but they only offer spots sponsored by schools

or companies. Not just anyone can join." He hung his head in his hands.

"If we can find what's happening to the jellyfish before we leave tomorrow, maybe you can still go," Ellie whispered.

Tink whipped his head up. "Then we need to find those jellyfish."

ACHOO!

A sneeze came from the dark forest, and to Ellie's shock and delight, Jessica stepped out and sat by the fire. Even though she sat far away, Ellie was still happy Jessica seemed to be feeling better.

"I think it is time for a spooky story before bed," said Miss Millotto, a short woman with gray hair and a twinkle in her eye. "I have been chaperoning this trip for a couple decades now, so I know a thing or two. Are you ready?"

The fire dimmed eerily.

"Once there was an old woman collecting mushrooms and berries in the forest around Jellyfish Lake. After little luck on her hunt, she finally stumbled upon a huge, juicy mushroom and was delighted that she would have

something to put in her soup. Except once the woman picked up the mushroom, she realized it wasn't a mushroom at all—it was a big, fat, hairy toe the size of her fist. With her stomach rumbling from hunger, she decided it would have to do and took it back to her small cabin on the edge of Jellyfish Lake."

"'That night, she made some soup with the giant toe and went to bed with a full stomach. But around midnight, the door to her cabin slowly opened. *CREAK*! And there stood a big hairy silhouette that was eight-feet-tall. The woman was never seen again, but there were footprints found in her cabin. Massive footprints with the left foot missing a big toe."

With a slightly shaky hand, Ellie reached into her backpack, pulled out a stick of Jelly Belly Liver Jam Jerky, and peeled back the wrapper. *It's just a story; it's not real. It's just a scary story*, she told herself.

Suddenly, the leaves on the round bush behind Ellie started to rustle.

Chapter Seven
Sloosh! Gurgle! Glug!

Ellie's heart pounded faster at the sound of the moving leaves. She tried to remind herself it was probably just a rabbit or a squirrel, but then something grabbed her ankle.

"EEK!" Ellie shrieked as she dropped her jerky.

POOF! She flew into a nearby tree.

Jack crawled out of the bush and laughed. "Such a Scaredy Bat!"

"What is wrong with you!?" shouted Jessica from the other side of the campfire.

"Yeah, don't you have anything better to do?" said Fez.

"Nothing is wrong with me. I'm hilarious. And the better question is, why can't you ever

get food in your mouth instead of on your shirt?" Jack pointed to the green stain left by the Liver Jam Jerky earlier.

Poof! Ellie transformed back into a vampire. "You're just a big bully!" she shouted.

"And you're just a wannabe vampire detective. You and your little friends will never solve

any real mysteries." Jack changed his voice as if he were talking to a baby. "Is little bitty Scaredy Bat scared again? Boohoo!"

Tink stood. "Hey, Grinko," he called in a voice that was a bit too quiet. When Jack couldn't hear over his maniacal laughter, Tink tried again in a louder voice. "Jack! Leave her alone. What did she ever do to you?"

Before Jack could answer, Mr. Bramble cut in. "Enough!" he yelled. "Why is it always this group that I have to deal with? Mr. Grinko—"

SLOOSH! GURGLE! GLUG! GLUG! A loud slurping sound echoed through the chilly night air.

Jack's face went pale. "Okay, that isn't me this time."

They looked down at the lake, which was now a large whirlpool with spinning water sloshing everywhere. Then, just as soon as the water vortex had started, it stopped, and the lake calmed into soft waves. The class broke out into a tidal wave of whispers and theories.

"Probably just an underwater spring or

something," assured Mr. Bramble. "Come along now; it's time for bed."

Jessica rushed to Ellie. "Does this have anything to do with the mystery you were telling me about?"

"Yes!" exclaimed Ellie. She explained about the jellyfish, what they had found so far, and how they needed to solve this so Tink could go

to Science Camp. "We need to get down there and look for clues," Ellie finished.

Tink and Fez both agreed, but Jessica remained silent.

"Do you think you're feeling well enough to join?" asked Ellie hopefully.

"Umm," said Jessica.

Fez picked up the Jelly Belly Liver Jam Jerky that Ellie had dropped when she turned into a bat. He looked at her with puppy dog eyes.

"Well, I'm not eating it," Ellie said, looking at the layer of dirt on it before turning her attention back to Jessica.

Fez blew it off, possibly releasing more spit than air.

Jessica stifled a sneeze. "No, I'll sit this one out," she finally answered.

Ellie's shoulders slumped as she watched Jessica take off down the hill. She'd thought for sure she was going to say yes. Fez shoved the rest of the jerky in his mouth and put a hand on Ellie's back.

"It's okay," he said. "Maybe she'll join us next time."

Ellie hoped he was right.

After the final headcount of the day, the three friends snuck down to the beach to search for more clues. They walked along the calm water's edge looking for anything out of the ordinary, but even with their flashlights and the light of the moon, it was hard to see.

"Ow," said Ellie as her foot hit something. A big long tooth was lying in the sand.

Chapter Eight
Footprints In The Sand

"Charybdis!" said Ellie. "I bet you she is behind this." Ellie stood at the calm lake that now had no signs of the whirlpool. Fez and Tink looked at her with blank stares.

"Who?" Tink asked.

"Charybdis," Ellie repeated. "She's a sea monster that makes giant whirlpools just by inhaling. Maybe she has been doing that and sucking up the jellyfish."

"Maybe," said Tink. "But this is a lake, not a sea."

"She visits lakes, too," Ellie explained. "I know Charybdis comes here because I see her in paparazzi photos on this beach all the

time. And look by my foot: this big long tooth is exactly like hers."

Fez squinted at the long, smooth fang lying on the beach. "You sure that's a tooth?"

"Of course!" said Ellie. She picked it up. "Just look how strong it is." She bent the tooth and it snapped in half, revealing splinters of wood.

"Or, it could be smooth beach wood," Tink said.

Ellie frowned. "Okay, that wasn't a tooth, but the whirlpool still sounds like Charybdis."

"Alright, so what kind of evidence would we need to prove that it was Charybdis?" Tink asked.

Ellie looked around the lake and thought.

"None," Fez said, to everyone's surprise.

Ellie slammed her eyebrows together. "Fez, a good detective *always* needs evidence. How else are we going to prove it?"

Fez unzipped Tink's backpack.

"Hey, what are you doing?" Tink asked.

"I know I put it in here somewhere," said Fez, reaching into the backpack. "Ah ha!" Fez yanked out a magazine.

"Um, that's not mine," Tink said.

"I know!" exclaimed Fez. "You always have your backpack, so sometimes I store things in there. I put this cooking magazine in just in case I wanted to read on the beach today."

"You just store stuff in my backpack!?"

"Yuppers!" Fez said with a huge grin.

Ellie giggled. "That's smart. But is now really the time to find a new recipe?"

Fez flipped through the magazine and finally stopped at a page near the back.

"No, look!" he said. Right there in the gossip section was a picture of Charybdis lying on a beach in Hawaii with her sunglasses and straw hat, sipping a fruit smoothie.

Ellie looked at the date on the photo. "That's only two days ago," Ellie calculated.

"Not nearly enough time to make it to Jellyfish Lake."

"Exactly!" exclaimed Fez. "I thought I saw that funny name somewhere recently. Did you know she has her own line of blenders?" Fez reached over to put his magazine back in the backpack, but Tink pulled away.

Tink squinted at Fez.

"Sorry, I'll ask next time," Fez assured Tink.

"Next time!?"

"Guys, I think we have something bigger to concentrate on than backpacks," Ellie exclaimed. She pointed to the giant footprints in the sand that led to the side of the lake. "I looked all over for footprints today and there is no way I would have missed ones this big. They must be new."

"Do you see what I see?" asked Tink.

"Of course, I'm the one that pointed out the footprints," Ellie said, a little annoyed he was trying to take credit. "Weren't you listening?"

"No, where they lead," Tink clarified. He raced to the thick oak tree and found a wooden cogwheel that blended in with the tree's trunk.

"If I am not mistaken..." Tink turned the cog by the handle, and the water started swirling, "I would say that this creates the whirlpools."

CLUNK!

The wheel stopped. Tink tried to continue turning it, but it was stuck.

"Oh well," he said. "We know what it does." He let go and wiped his hands on his pants.

"That's a great find!" complimented Ellie. "How did you spot that?"

"I could see the metal wire shining in the moonlight," Tink explained.

Ellie frowned. "I completely missed that..." She let out a heavy breath. "Maybe Jack is right and I will never be a real detective. How could I miss that?"

"Don't listen to Jack," insisted Fez. "He's just a big bully."

Ellie laughed, then reached in her trench coat pocket and pulled out her notebook. "Funny you should say that!" she said as she flipped to the page she had been working on earlier. She tapped on where she'd written about Jack being a bully.

1. *~~Pollution~~ – (The water tested fine and the frog wasn't dead.)*
2. *~~Jack~~ – (The jellyfish went missing before he arrived. But he's still a big bully!)*
3. *Someone that needs the jellyfish for something… but who?*

Ellie ran her finger over the last line of her notebook entry. That was it!

"I think someone used the cogwheel to steal the jellyfish!" Ellie exclaimed. "We just have to figure out who." She turned her attention to the footprints. "These turn and go toward the forest. I bet if we follow them, we can find the jellyfish thief."

Chapter Nine

Cabin in the Woods

Ellie, Tink, and Fez followed the giant footsteps to an old cabin not too far into the woods. All three of them stood at the warped wood door, bugs crawling about the nooks and crannies. Ellie watched a spider scurry by, plucked it off, and popped it in her mouth.

CRUNCH! CRUNCH!

"That will never not gross me out," Tink said with a gag. They peered into a window beside the door, but there were no lights, and the window was caked with filth. They couldn't see anything.

CREAK! Fez had his hand on the door, and both Ellie and Tink shushed him at the same time.

"Sorry," Fez whispered. "But the door wasn't even shut." After one last look in the dirty window, they decided to go in. The floorboards squeaked and creaked as they tiptoed through the door into the small one-room cabin. They shone their flashlights around to find furniture covered in white sheets that had turned grey from filth and shelves of books covered in layers of thick dust. The air felt heavy with the stench of molded wood and mothballs.

"Looks like it's abandoned," Tink whispered. A brown rat ran across the floor with a small squeak. "Well, almost abandoned."

"It's so cute!" Fez declared, trying to find exactly where it had run to.

Ellie shuddered as the critter scurried under the desk in the corner. She had an urge to bolt out of the cabin, but she knew they needed to solve this mystery to save Jellyfish Lake. She picked up an old magnifying glass off a small wooden table and blew the dust off. She raised it to her face and squinted at the room through the lens. She loved how big everything appeared through a magnifying glass. The rat

ran to the other side of the room, and it looked like a giant monster, making Ellie jump.

"Do you think that maybe that bus driver just saw a rat or other rodent on the road?" asked Ellie after some thought.

"A giant rat?" asked Tink.

"No, a normal-sized one. But maybe it just

looked huge through his thick glasses. Like looking through a magnifying glass." Ellie placed the magnifying glass back on the table.

"Maybe," said Tink. "But if that's the case, I really hope he isn't our driver on the way home."

Ellie was looking at Fez trying to lure the rat out from a crack in the wall when she spotted something. The rat left behind little footprints on the dirty floor wherever it ran. She shone her flashlight behind her. She was leaving footprints too—the floor was that dirty. However, there was one path on the floor that was almost like a trail. It had much less dirt. As if the dust was worn away.

Ellie followed the trail to a bookshelf. There were lots of odd little knick-knacks like porcelain clowns, trinket boxes, and toy cars scattered among the many books. As she scanned the dozen shelves, one trinket box stood out from the rest. It wasn't anything special, just a silver heart with a rose on top, but it was the only thing on the whole shelf that wasn't dusty. Ellie tried to lift the box, but it wouldn't budge,

so instead, she opened it. Inside was a red button. She took a deep breath and jabbed it with her finger. The bookcase beside her swung open with a thump. Fez and Tink both turned.

"How did you do that!?" Tink asked.

Ellie gave a big fanged smile. She couldn't believe she did it.

"Do you guys remember the episode of *The Amazing Vampire Detective* when Hailey Haddie

found the diamonds?" Fez and Tink nodded, so Ellie continued. "She found them because the book that opened the hiding spot was the only thing that didn't have dust on it." Ellie pointed to the box before waving for them to go with her through the door.

The trio peered into the secret passageway and found a dimly lit staircase going down.

Ellie gulped. "You two first," she whispered.

"Why do we have to go first?" Fez complained.

"Because I found the hidden door."

The two boys couldn't argue with that, so they stepped down the first few stairs, followed by Ellie, and one very unexpected guest. To Fez's delight, the rat that they had seen earlier followed them onto the stairs. Fez let out a tiny squeal when he spotted the little critter. He wanted to be friends with every animal he met.

Fez ran back up the stairs, passed Ellie, and managed to corner the rat on one of the steps.

"Don't worry, little guy, I don't want to hurt you," he assured his new furry friend as he

scooped him off the wooden step. "Oh, that's a cute sweater. Wait… why are you wearing a leopard-print sweater?"

ACHOO!

"Sanalamia, Fez," said Ellie as she squinted to try to see what might be at the bottom of the stairs.

"Umm, that wasn't me," said Fez. Ellie and Tink turned around to see Jessica in Fez's arms.

Chapter Ten

Rat, Bat, Cat, or Worm

"Jessica!?" Ellie cried. "Where did you come from?"

"And how did you just appear?" Tink added.

Jessica hopped out of Fez's arms, and the secret door slammed shut. Her leopard-print sweater had caught on a red lever. "Oops," Jessica said with a quivering lip as she unhooked her sweater. Tink ran up the stairs and lifted the lever, but the door didn't budge. All Ellie could do was stand on the stairs with her mouth open. She couldn't believe her eyes.

"This isn't reopening the door!" Tink cried, giving it one last tug.

"Forget about that!" Ellie snapped. "Where

did you come from?" she asked Jessica once again.

"I got my transformational powers. And can you guess what I am?" Jessica's eyes filled with tears. "I couldn't be something cool and classic like a bat, I had to be— I had to be,—"

Ellie gasped. "You're a rat!"

Jessica burst into tears. "I'm a gross brown rat. And now you won't want to be my friend anymore. I tried being mean to you so you wouldn't want to be friends and would never have to find out, but now you know." Jessica sat down on the step, put her head in her hands, and sobbed. Ellie walked up the steps and gave her best friend a hug.

"Jess, I will always be your friend. I don't care if you're a rat. I'm actually excited, because now we get to deal with transformational powers together."

Jessica sniffled. "But how can you be my friend if you're scared of me? You're scared of everything."

Ellie giggled. "Well, yeah, I'm scared of a lot, but I could never be scared of you." Ellie

thought back to earlier, when the rat that was presumably Jessica had run across her foot. "Earlier at the beach, I was just startled," Ellie explained. "I'll always be your friend. Whether you're a rat, bat, cat, or worm."

Jessica's eyes widened. "Oh, thank goodness I am not a worm!" Both girls laughed.

"Do you guys still want to be my friend, even if I'm a gross rat?" asked Jessica with a lip tremble as she turned to Fez and Tink.

"Dude, I think that's awesome!" said Fez. "You're adorable as a rat!"

Jessica stood and put her hand on her hips. "Are you saying I'm not adorable as a vampire?"

Fez's face dropped. "No… I just think animals are extra cute."

"I have a question," announced Tink.

Jessica groaned. "No, I can't control it. For some reason, sneezes seem to trigger the transformation. I guess kind of like being scared triggers it for Ellie. But unlike her, I can't turn into a rat or vampire on command. Only when I sneeze. Then once I'm a rat, I have to sneeze again to turn back."

"Actually, I was going to ask, if I build a rat maze in the lab, will you test-run it for me?" Tink said in a soft voice.

"No! Absolutely not," Jessica bellowed as she threw her hands in the air.

Tink looked at Fez and shrugged. "It was worth a try."

"Thanks, guys," Jessica said with a smile. "Does this mean we can solve this mystery now?"

They all cheered.

They walked down the stairs and found themselves in a large cave with flickers of blue light dancing on the walls. Right in the middle, there was a large pool of turquoise water. The water was moving, and soon it became clear what the deep pool contained.

"The jellyfish!" Fez cried. "Look how cute and squidgy they are."

"There must be thousands of them here," Jessica added.

"We did it!" said Tink with a fist pump in the air. The four friends high-fived and it echoed throughout the cave. Then they all put their fingers to their lips. "Shhh!"

"But who is behind this?" Jessica asked. "I was worried about you guys, so I've been following you as a rat since Fez made me sneeze

by blowing dirt at me from ground beef jerky." She squinted at Fez.

"It was Jelly Belly Liver Jam Jerky. NOT beef jerky," Fez corrected.

"Either way, it was dirty ground jerky. Anyway, my point is, I know you followed some big footprints from the beach. Do you think whoever those footprints belong to stole the jellyfish?"

"Yes, but that's all we know," Ellie confirmed. Ellie wandered to a corner of the cave with papers stuck to the wall. There was a fridge running off a generator in the corner and a bunch of bowls, jars, and spoons spread out across a counter.

"Come here," she told everyone. She pointed to a recipe taped to the wall titled *Secret Recipe*. There were lots of ingredients scratched out in black ink.

"You're the food expert," Ellie said to Fez. "What do you think?" Ellie opened the fridge and found dozens of jars of jam. But not just any jam: glowing jam.

Fez scratched his chin. "Seems to be some

sort of weird jam. But who makes jam with jellyfish?"

"I do!" came a loud voice from behind them.

The friends whirled around to see a ginormous furry creature emerge from the pool of water. The wet brown fur that covered his entire eight-foot-tall body dripped onto his giant feet. They had finally found the jellyfish thief—and he was much bigger than any of them had imagined.

POOF!

Secret Recipe

Chapter Eleven

Jelly Belly

"Hey, you guys look familiar," said the humongous furry monster. "Aren't you that little detective team that saved the Royal Wedding?"

Tink, Fez, and Jessica silently nodded.

POOF! Ellie transformed back into a vampire and nodded as well.

"Neat trick!" the creature said. He walked toward the group and held out his hand. "I'm Bigfoot, pleased to meet you!" One by one, they all shook his ginormous thumb.

"Gee, you guys sure are quiet now," Bigfoot said. "You were a lot louder when you had your whole rat conversation on the stairs."

"Hey, that was a private conversation!" Jessica exclaimed.

"Ah, so you guys do still talk," Bigfoot said.

"We're just kind of shocked," Tink said. "I didn't think you existed."

Bigfoot patted down his wet fur. "Last time I checked, I did."

Tink gave a small smile.

"I knew you existed," said Ellie, "but I never expected you to be able to talk."

Bigfoot let out a laugh that boomed and echoed through the cave. "Fair enough; I know there are a lot of weird stories about me. The worst is probably that one where the lady makes soup with my toe."

"Wait, that was true!?" Fez asked.

"Kind of. I did lose my big toe, but no woman found it and ate it. A good lesson to be careful with an ax, though." Bigfoot chuckled. "I guess you could say I had an ax-ccident." Everyone giggled this time. While Bigfoot was nothing like any of them had imagined, they could all agree he was really friendly, and quite funny.

Ellie thought back to the footsteps and didn't

remember a toe missing. She looked down at his big hairy feet and counted ten toes.

"If you lost a toe, why do you have ten?" Ellie questioned.

Bigfoot reached down and, with a small pop, pulled off his big toe.

"This one is just a prosthetic! I am quite

the craftsman when it comes to putting things together. Well, except recipes, apparently."

"That's because you're not supposed to put cute and squishy jellyfish in jam!" Fez scolded.

"I actually haven't yet. I've tried everything but can't get the recipe exactly right. The release of Jelly Belly Glowing Jelly is next month, and I figured jellyfish were squishy, so maybe they would work."

Fez's jaw dropped. "You're behind Jelly Belly Liver Jam Jerky!?"

"Sure am!" said Bigfoot, rubbing his stomach. "Who else has a jelly belly like me?" He gave his stomach a shake, and it jiggled like a bowl of gelatin.

"I LOVE your jerky," gushed Fez.

"Glad you like it. That fridge back there has a whole shelf at the bottom, so help yourself," offered Bigfoot. Fez's eyes grew wide, and he gladly accepted.

"You need to release these jellyfish back into the lake," Ellie told Bigfoot. "If you don't, they are going to have to close the park."

"And cancel the summer camp!" Tink added.

"Oh my, I had no idea," said Bigfoot. "But I need the jellyfish for my jelly." He turned back to look at the pool's flickering blue water.

"What if we could fix your jam without using the jellyfish?" asked Jessica.

"Then that would be a deal!" said Bigfoot.

"While you're at it, you should change your packaging," Ellie added. "Your wrappers are all over the beach."

"Noted," Bigfoot said. "I am actually working on compostable packaging."

"Great!" exclaimed Ellie. "Then let's do this so we can go back to our cabins."

Bigfoot opened the fridge and retrieved a bright blue jar of jam with a blackberry label.

"This one has plenty of glow, but it tastes kind of funny," Bigfoot explained. He unscrewed the lid and handed everyone a spoon. The whole gang slurped up their spoonful and then made faces like they'd just sucked on lemons.

"Why is it so sour!?" Fez asked through puckered cheeks.

"The solution I use to make it glow turns everything sour and bitter." Bigfoot yanked

open a drawer and pulled out a small vial of Neo Glo. Jessica opened the Neo Glo and took a sniff.

"Ick! I can see why," Jessica announced. "Smells like rotten limes and stinky cheese." She handed it to Tink, who scanned the ingredient list.

"Did you try putting more sugar in the recipe?" Fez asked.

"Sure did," Bigfoot said. "Still wasn't good." Bigfoot grabbed another jar from the fridge. This one also had a blackberry label but was more of a dark purple color. Once again, everyone took a bite, but this time they instantly spit it out. Bigfoot groaned. "So, it is as bad as I think."

"Possibly worse," said Jessica as she wiped her tongue on her arm.

"How does that glow stuff make everything taste so bad?" Ellie asked.

Bigfoot looked at the floor, then the ceiling. "Um, well, that one doesn't even have the Neo Glo. That was my base recipe..."

Ellie's face turned bright red. "I just meant that it has a very unique taste."

Bigfoot laughed. "No, it tastes awful. I just can't figure out how to make good jam consistently. Even the batches that turn out okay get ruined with the taste of Neo Glo."

"What if I could isolate the glow and take out some of the bitter taste?" Tink inquired as he looked over the Neo Glo ingredients.

"That would be awesome!" said Bigfoot. "But it won't make the bad batches of jam good."

"No, but we know someone who is a great cook," said Ellie.

"Someone who could teach you," Jessica added. Everyone looked toward Fez, who was now digging in the fridge. He closed the door and found everyone silently staring at him.

"Me?" Fez asked.

"Of course!" said Ellie.

"Oh! I would be happy to help!" Fez said as he unwrapped a stick of jerky. "But as soon as I get the taste of the last jelly out of my mouth."

Everyone agreed that was a great idea.

After a quick snack, hours of cooking, and a pile of dishes almost as tall as Bigfoot, they did it! They had a glowing jam. It didn't taste sour. It didn't taste bad. In fact, it tasted amazing. Like a bowl of ripe berries sprinkled with sugar.

"Thank you so much!" said Bigfoot. "I owe you guys big time."

"No problem," Ellie said. "This has been a lot of fun!" Everyone nodded in agreement. "We should get going, though," Ellie added with a yawn.

"We should definitely go," Tink agreed. "It must be really late!"

"Umm, just one problem," said Bigfoot as everyone started for the stairs. "We are kind of trapped in here."

"What do you mean?" asked Ellie.

"You guys sure do like to touch things. When you hit the red lever on the stairs, you put the place on lockdown. That usually wouldn't be a problem, but you also turned that cogwheel on the tree and jammed the emergency exit in

the pool that leads to the lake. I could only pry it open a crack."

"We're stuck?" asked Jessica.

Bigfoot nodded. "We're stuck."

Chapter Twelve

Ready Yeti

They were stuck in a cave with Bigfoot. If they couldn't get out, they would be in big trouble when their teacher discovered they were missing. And it may be too late for Jellyfish Lake.

"Isn't there a way to undo the lockdown?" Tink asked in disbelief.

"Nope," said Bigfoot. "It's a fairly new system, so it still has some kinks."

Jessica looked at the pool that contained the jellyfish and the small work area.

"What on earth would you need a lockdown for? If someone steals back the jellyfish? There isn't much in here."

Bigfoot squinted. "Yeti."

"Yeti?" all four asked in unison.

"Wait, isn't that just another name for you?" Fez asked.

"No!" Bigfoot roared. "I am so tired of people thinking I am the same as that—as that furry fraud. I am smart enough to make my own snack creations, but him, well..." Bigfoot exhaled hard. "He is always trying to rip me off. Like his newest product, 'Ready Yeti Kidney Jam Jerky.'" Bigfoot grunted. "Clearly a huge rip-off!" He let out a roar of frustration that shook the cave. The detective squad backed away from the furry beast.

"Sorry," Bigfoot apologized, as they stared at him wide-eyed. "I just can't stand him and how he treats me." Bigfoot took a deep breath. "I know it's best not to let him get to me and to ignore his shenanigans. But it's hard sometimes. He really knows how to push my buttons! Surely, you know someone like that and understand."

Jack flashed through Ellie's mind—she knew all too well.

Ellie changed the topic. "Okay, but we need to get out of here soon, or we'll be in a lot of

trouble, and a bunch of people will be very worried."

Bigfoot shrugged. "Sorry, little vampire, the emergency exit is jammed, so there is only a tiny crack." Bigfoot scratched his chin. "However… If I pry it open a little more, someone small could fit through. Then, if they go back to the bookcase and push the button, we could all get out."

Ellie looked at Tink, who was clearly the smallest out of the five of them. "Looks like you have some swimming to do."

Bigfoot shook his head. "No, the opening is much smaller than him… more like, oh, I don't know. Bat-sized."

A lump settled in Ellie's throat. There was no way she was swimming in that deep water, especially with all those jellyfish. "Jessica's a rat!" she blabbed, trying to pass off the task.

"Ellie, I can only transform when I sneeze," Jessica said with a sigh.

Ellie frantically grabbed some dirt off the ground and threw it at Jessica.

"Ellie!" Jessica shrieked. "What are you

doing?" Jessica grabbed some dirt and threw it back.

Ellie coughed and stuck out her tongue. "I was just trying to get you to sneeze."

"I can't do this for you," Jessica said as she shook the dirt out of her red curls and wiped her hands on her dress. "Only you can. Just think of how much trouble we are going to be in if we don't get out of here and how sad Hailey Haddie would be if her favorite vacation spot closed—"

"And about my Science Camp!" Tink interrupted.

"And yes, Tink's Science Camp," Jessica repeated. She looked over at Tink. "I was getting there."

"But I don't think I can do it," Ellie said in a small voice. Ellie kicked a small pebble, and it skipped across the cave floor. Her stomach felt like it had hundreds of butterflies fluttering around in it.

"What if we swim with you as far as we can?" Jessica offered as she took Ellie's hand and gave it a squeeze.

Ellie looked up at her three best friends, all nodding in agreement. When she went on this field trip, she'd expected to have fun and maybe meet Hailey Haddie—if she was lucky—not to have the fate of Jellyfish Lake depend on her. She took in a deep breath, puffed out her cheeks, and blew out a big exhale. If there was ever a time to prove she was more than a Scaredy Bat, it was now.

"Okay," Ellie finally agreed. "Let's do this."

Chapter Thirteen
Little Ballerinas

Ellie stood at the edge of the pool filled with jellyfish and watched them gently gliding around the water.

"Are you sure they can't hurt me?" Ellie asked for the fifth time.

"Positive!" Tink reassured her. "The fact that this type of jellyfish doesn't sting is what makes Jellyfish Lake so popular."

Ellie rubbed the goosebumps on her arms. "Alright, then let's get this over with."

Bigfoot went over the plan one more time. "I am going to pry open the door; then I need you guys to jam my fake toe in it to make sure it doesn't close before Ellie is out." He reached down to his massive furry foot, popped off his

fake big toe once again, and offered it to Jessica.

"No way!" Jessica squealed, putting her hands behind her back.

Fez gladly grabbed the giant toe. "This is so cool," he declared. With the toe firmly placed under his arm, he lined up on the water's edge with everyone else.

"Ready?" shouted Bigfoot. "Five, four, three…"

Ellie took the deepest breath she could and clenched her eyes shut.

"Two, one."

SPLASH!

The chill of the water enveloped her whole body. All she could see was blackness, but then she remembered her eyes were still shut. She opened them and things started coming into focus. Everyone was swimming toward the bottom of the pool. Jellyfish swam around each side of her, and a bright pink one circled her head before gliding down and tickling her leg with its tentacles. Ellie gave a small smile. The smack of jellyfish looked like little ballerinas

moving in slow motion, with their wispy tentacles waving about and the gentle sway of their bodies—they were beautiful.

Ellie looked down at Jessica, waving at her to come to the bottom of the pool. She was surprised when she found herself wishing she could stay longer with the jellyfish. Multiple jellyfish brushed against her as she swam to the bottom.

She arrived just in time. Bigfoot pried open the metal door so Fez could jam the big toe in.

TUNK!

The door slammed down over the toe, leaving a tiny opening. Ellie got a big hairy thumbs-up and knew this was her moment.

POOF!

She transformed into a bat, flapped her wings, and zipped through the small opening into the weedy bottom of the lake. Ellie's bat wings made great flippers—she was able to propel herself around quicker than usual.

Just breathe, she reminded herself. *No, wait! Don't do that! You'll inhale water. Just relax and keep flapping.*

She zigged and zagged through the weedy bottom until the light of the moon was visible. Quickly, she started flapping to the surface, but she wasn't going anywhere. A weed had wrapped itself around her leg and was keeping her at the bottom of the lake.

She reached down to try to untangle herself, but her small bat hands were no use.

This can't be happening! Why didn't I pay more attention when my Dad taught me about tying and untying knots? she silently fretted.

Next, she tried to transform back into a vampire, but it didn't work. She needed to concentrate on transforming, and she was panicking too much. The air in her lungs was quickly disappearing. A few bubbles escaped her mouth as she gave a big tug.

Jellyfish swam around her as she frantically tried to free her foot, but none seemed to notice her struggle. Until the bright pink one appeared. It wrapped its tentacles under the weed and, with one big tug, Ellie was finally free. She flew to the surface and rocketed out of the water into the night sky.

The fresh forest air never felt so good.

Chapter Fourteen
Wishes And Dreams

The four friends sat on the cool beach sand and watched the sun creep over the horizon.

"And then after I made it out of the water, getting to the button to open the door for you guys was no problem," Ellie explained as she tried to stifle a yawn.

Jessica gasped. "I can't believe you got stuck! Are you sure you're okay?"

"Yeah, I'm sure," Ellie reassured her. "I was lucky that jellyfish was there to help me, though. I had no idea they were so smart."

"But they're not really," said Tink. "Don't get me wrong, they're fascinating creatures,

but understanding someone is in danger and helping, well, that is just odd."

"Not as odd as Jessica being a rat." Fez pointed to the rat-shaped birthmark on Jessica's arm and gave it a poke. "Look how cute it is," he teased. Jessica covered the spot with her hand and narrowed her eyes at him.

"Alright, explain this to me one more time," said Tink.

Jessica threw her head back. "Ellie, I can't explain this again, it's your turn."

Ellie smiled at the thought of Jessica already explaining this to the boys three times. "Okay, so some vampires have birthmarks that show which animal they transform into. But the birthmark only appears once their transformational powers kick in."

"It's not technically a birthmark if you haven't had it since you were born," scoffed Tink.

"It looks like one, so that's what it's called," Ellie explained. "I don't make the rules. Anyway, I don't have one because my dad is human and only full vampires get them."

"And this is a big secret?" Fez asked.

"Yes. When vampires weren't accepted, often we would transform into our animal form to hide. My parents said humans still don't know we can turn into other animals besides bats. And they definitely don't know full vampires have marks that show what animal they transform into," explained Ellie.

"It's a big secret because our transformations are what will keep us safe in case we ever have to go into hiding again," Jessica added. "So you can't tell anyone!"

"We won't," promised both boys.

Ellie looked back at the calm lake. A woodpecker tapped against a tree not too far away.

"I can't believe I did it," she said with a small smile as she thought about the crazy night they'd had. She looked over at her three best friends. "I can't believe *we* did it," she corrected.

With their help, Bigfoot had figured out how to make his glowing jelly taste great—all without using jellyfish. So, he promised to release all the jellyfish and sort everything out with the park rangers. Jellyfish Lake was saved thanks to the little detective team.

Even though they couldn't tell anyone about their adventure without getting in heaps of trouble for sneaking out, they were happy to keep the experience between them. Ellie was thrilled to have solved another mystery, while Jessica was simply content to have her friends

by her side. Fez was enthusiastically munching on the unlimited supply of Jelly Belly Liver Jam Jerky Bigfoot offered as thanks for helping with the recipe. And Tink, well, Tink may have been the most excited of all. He couldn't stop talking about how Bigfoot offered him a spot at the Jellyfish Lake Science Camp.

It turned out that Bigfoot reserved a few camp spots every year for kids that his company sponsored. And after talking to Tink about the science behind Jelly Belly's recipes, he knew Tink deserved a spot.

"I just can't believe I get to go to Science Camp!" Tink squealed.

"We know, we know," said Jessica. "Can't you talk about anything else?"

"No way!" exclaimed Tink. "You're going to be hearing about this forever. This is my dream come true."

Jessica groaned, and Ellie chuckled. Just as Ellie thought nothing could ruin the bliss she felt, a familiar voice came from behind her.

"Aw, is Scaredy Bat and her wannabe detective squad too scared to go swimming?" Jack

taunted. With a cackle, he threw his bag down and ran into the lake.

Ellie balled her hands into fists by her side.

"I am getting so sick of him!" she exploded. "I wish he really would turn purple."

"Don't let him get to you," Jessica said. "Bigfoot was right. We should just ignore him when he's trying to bother us."

Ellie knew she was right, but sometimes that felt impossible.

A few minutes later, the sun was fully out, and Jack ran back to shore and popped his sunscreen out of his bag. He began slathering the thick lotion over his face, and to Ellie's surprise—and delight—it was purple!

Ellie's mouth dropped open as Jack's face turned the color of a grape. He started rubbing more on his arms and then looked down.

"What is this!?" he cried, looking at the purple goop. Jack glared at Tink. "Did you do this?"

Tink shook his head.

Jack tried to wipe his hands on his swim trunks, but they were stained purple. He ran

back into the lake and frantically splashed water over his face and arms, but nothing happened. Jack came out of the lake, huffing and puffing.

"Mr. Bramble!" he cried as he ran to the cabins.

"Tink, you're a genius!" Jessica laughed.

"It really wasn't me this time!" exclaimed Tink.

Ellie giggled. "I guess some wishes do come true."

Fez shut his eyes. "I wish for a pet llama." He opened his eyes and looked around the beach, but there was no llama in sight. He slumped his shoulders. "It was worth a try."

Ellie hopped to her feet. "You guys ready?" Everyone else followed, and they raced into the lake. But after only a few minutes of splashing and playing, Ellie got her necklace caught in her hair.

"Be right back!" Ellie called to her friends as she rushed to shore. Her chain was wrapped around a big chunk of her hair. Ellie tugged on it, but it was really twisted in there.

A sloshing sound came from the shore, and Ellie caught a glimpse of pink from Jessica's swimsuit coming out of the water.

"Jess, can you help me?" Ellie asked. Jessica came over and helped her untangle the necklace. Once the purple dragon pendant was safely in her bag, Ellie turned around to thank Jessica. But it wasn't Jessica at all.

Ellie gasped. It was Hailey Haddie!

Hailey gave a small wave and smiled as she walked past. Too shocked to form words, all Ellie could do was watch her hero walk up the beach. And that was when she saw it. The jellyfish-shaped birthmark on Hailey Haddie's ankle.

Chapter Fifteen

An Invitation

Dear Ellie,

I know all the work you did to save Jellyfish Lake and I can't thank you enough! It is the one place in the world I can go to "blend in" and be normal for a while. I don't know what I would do without it, and I don't know what the world would do without budding detectives like you—you and your friends make a great team!

Speaking of detective work, I know on the beach that you noticed my birthmark, and I beg you and your friends... please don't tell anyone. I'm counting on you to keep my biggest secret.

I would like to invite you all to my movie filming in Brookside next month to thank you personally. The set passes are enclosed. In the meantime, I thought

you might enjoy an advance copy of my latest book.

See you on set!

With love and gratitude,

Hailey Haddie

Ellie's hand shook, causing the letter to tremble like a leaf as she read it out loud to her friends. She couldn't believe it. Not only did her all-time hero Hailey Haddie know she existed, but Hailey also sent her a personal letter, an advance copy of her book, *and* an invitation to go on set. Ellie's mouth gaped, and her heart hammered against her chest.

"Did Hailey Haddie just invite us all to her movie set?" Jessica asked in disbelief.

Tink nodded. "It would seem she did."

Ellie let out a loud squeal and began dancing around and singing, "I'm going to see Hailey Haddie again! I'm going to see Hailey Haddie again!"

Jessica put her hands on her hips and loudly cleared her throat.

Ellie paused for a couple of seconds, looked at her friends, and then restarted her song and dance. "*We're* going to see Hailey Haddie.

We're going to see Hailey Haddie!" Jessica, Tink, and Fez joined in. They hopped around the room, fantasizing about what being on the movie set would be like and disagreeing on what the best part would be.

"I hear they have a great special effects department," said Tink.

"Ooo, movie sets always have the best food!"

said Fez with a glimmer of excitement in his eye.

"Oh, Fez." Jessica let out a short giggle. "I can't wait to visit the costume department. It's always my favorite part of visiting my mom's movie sets." She smiled at Ellie. "What are you the most excited about?"

Everyone laughed, because they knew that question needed no answer.

While the four friends were excited about their set invitation for different reasons, they could all agree on one thing—it was going to be a blast.

Everyone left shortly after, and Ellie lay on her pink coffin bed with Hailey Haddie's book, *How to Be the World's Greatest Detective: A Step-by-Step Guide to Solving Mysteries*. But before she could crack it open, her pesky sister Penny sauntered in.

"Whatcha reading, Scaredy Bat?" Penny asked.

"Get out of my room!" Ellie shouted.

"Okay," said Penny, to Ellie's surprise. Then she grabbed the book and ran.

"Get back here, you little brat," Ellie screamed. She caught up to Penny at the end of the hall, tackled her to the ground, and snatched the book.

"Ow! I'm telling Mom!" Penny threatened. "And I saw what you were reading. A Scaredy Bat like you will never be a real detective." With a quivering lip, Penny ran downstairs. "Mom! Ellie jumped on me!"

Ellie took in a deep breath and made her way back into her room, this time making sure to close the door. But as she climbed back on her bed with her book, her excitement wasn't the same. What Penny had said was much like the words Jack taunted her with—that Scaredy Bats couldn't be real detectives. She thought of the mysteries she'd solved, but what if those didn't count? She ran her finger over the title of the book and figured it was as good a place as any to start building her detective skills.

She cracked the thick book open to the first page and took a deep inhale of the fresh pages. She knew she would cherish this book forever, but the inscription on the second page

scribbled in gold ink was just the icing on the cake.

Ellie,

"Great detectives aren't born; they're made. May this book help you become the best you can be... And never forget, believing in yourself goes a long way."

Hailey Haddie

Being a Scaredy Bat certainly wasn't always easy, but Ellie knew she was doing her best. As for proving she was a real detective, well, that could wait until another day.

Hi!

Did you enjoy the mystery?

I know I did!

If you want to join the team as we solve more mysteries, then leave a review!

Otherwise, we won't know if you're up for the next mystery. And when we go to solve it, you may never get to hear about it!

You can **leave a review** on Amazon, Goodreads, or wherever else you found the book.

The gang and I are excited to see you in the next mystery adventure!

Fingers crossed there's nothing scary in that one...

The mysterious adventures of Ellie Spark in

Scaredy Bat

Also by Marina J. Bowman:
The Legend of Pineapple Cove

To learn more, visit marinajbowman.com

Don't miss Book #4 in the

Scaredy Bat series!

Pre-Order Now!

scaredybat.com/book4

Are You Afraid of Deep Water?

Thalassophobia [thah-lah-sow-fow-bee-uh] is the intense and persistent fear of deep, dark bodies of water such as the ocean. It comes from "thalassa," the Greek word for sea and "phobos," the Greek word for fear.

Fear Rating: Thalassophobia is one of the somewhat common phobias. People with this

phobia can experience a racing heart, rapid breathing, sweating, nausea, and dizziness.

Origin: Fear of deep water comes from an instinctual evolutionary response, a traumatic past experience, the unknown depths, and media portrayals.

Fear Facts:

- Water creatures are more afraid of you or have no interest (even sharks).
- 95% of sea animals are invertebrates (no backbone) like jellyfish & shrimp.
- Slimy seaweed is a main ingredient in sushi, ice cream, shampoo, toothpaste and makeup. It also produces up to 70% of the world's oxygen.
- Humans are made to float! You can also bring a floaty for more buoyancy.
- Tips: practice in pools, bring friends, play games, and focus on the beauty.

Jokes: How do you make a shark laugh?
Tell a whale of a tale!

Fear No More! With some caution, deep bodies of water like oceans and lakes are safe and fun. But if you believe you suffer from thalassophobia and want help, talk to your parents or doctor about treatment options. For more fear facts, visit: scaredybat.com/book3bonus.

Suspect List

Fill in the suspects as you read, and don't worry if they're different from Ellie's suspects. When you think you've solved the mystery, fill out the "who did it" section on the next page!

Name: Write the name of your suspect

Motive: Write the reason why your suspect might have committed the crime

Access: Write the time and place you think it could have happened

How: Write the way they could have done it

Clues: Write any observations that may support the motive, access, or how

Suspect 1

Draw below

Name:
Motive:
Access:
How:
Clues:

Suspect 2

Draw below

Name:
Motive:
Access:
How:
Clues:

Suspect 3

Draw below

Name:
Motive:
Access:
How:
Clues:

Suspect 4

Draw below

Name:
Motive:
Access:
How:
Clues:

Who Did It?

Now that you've identified all of your suspects, it's time to use deductive reasoning to figure out who actually committed the crime! Remember, the suspect must have a strong desire to commit the crime (or cause the accident) and the ability to do so.

For more detective fun, visit:
scaredybat.com/book3bonus

Name:
Motive:
Access:
How:
Clues:

Hidden Details Observation Sheet -- Level One --

1. Where did Ellie and her classmates visit for their school trip?
2. What did the bus driver see that made him slam on the breaks?
3. What sticky substance did Ellie step in by the lake?
4. What "dead" creature did the kids find that was actually sleeping?
5. What supposed "clue" did Ellie find at night on the beach?
6. Whose footprints did Ellie, Fez, and Tink follow to the cabin in the woods?
7. With her new transformation powers, what kind of animal does Jessica turn into?
8. What did Bigfoot need the jellyfish for?
9. Who or what helped Ellie when she got tangled in seaweed as a bat?
10. What color did Jack mysteriously turn at the end of the story?

Hidden Details Observation Sheet

-- Level Two --

1. What is the name of the snack company that Ellie got her jerky from?
2. What prize did Mr. Bramble announce on the bus for the best project?
3. Who or what grabbed Ellie's ankle when they were sitting around the campfire?
4. What device created the whirlpool that sucked up the jellyfish?
5. What supernatural creature did Ellie suspect was taking the jellyfish?
6. Where did Ellie find the button to open the secret door behind the bookcase?
7. What was the rat wearing in the cabin in the woods?
8. What is the name of Jelly Belly's competitor business?
9. What did the kids use to prop open the emergency exit at the bottom of the pool?
10. What does Hailey have on her ankle?

Hidden Details Observation Sheet
-- Level Three --

1. What is the title of the book Tink reads on the bus ride?
2. What historical treaty was signed on the beaches of Jellyfish Lake?
3. Who is Tink's hero?
4. What does Ellie say when someone sneezes?
5. When they hear the lake will have to close, what prize did Mr. Bramble announce instead?
6. What did Fez store in Tink's backpack that helped them clear Charybdis of the crime?
7. How did Bigfoot actually lose his toe?
8. Why doesn't Ellie have a bat shaped birth-mark?
9. What did Fez wish for?
10. What is the title of the book Hailey gave to Ellie?

For more detective fun, visit:
scaredybat.com/book3bonus

Answer Key

Level One Answers

1. Jellyfish Lake
2. A big furry monster
3. Orange soda
4. A frog
5. A tooth / beach wood
6. Bigfoot's
7. A brown rat
8. To make jam
9. A pink jellyfish / Hailey Haddie
10. Purple

Level Two Answers

1. Jelly Belly
2. Tickets to Science Camp
3. Jack
4. A wooden cogwheel
5. Charybdis
6. Silver heart shaped box with a rose on top
7. A leopard print sweater / Jessica's sweater
8. Ready Yeti
9. Bigfoot's prosthetic toe
10. A jellyfish birthmark

Level Three Answers

1. The Wonders of Jellyfish Lake
2. The Fang and Flesh Treaty
3. Bonnie Samson
4. Sanalamia
5. Mega Adventure Land amusement park
6. A cooking magazine
7. In an ax-ccident
8. Because her dad is human and only full vampires get them
9. A pet llama
10. How to Be the World's Greatest Detective: A Step-by-Step Guide to Solving Mysteries

Questions for Discussion

1. What did you enjoy about this book?
2. What are some of the themes of this story?
3. How did the characters use their strengths to solve the mystery together?
4. What is another way Ellie and her friends could have handled Jack's bullying?
5. What fears did the characters express in the book? When have you been afraid? How have you dealt with your fears?
6. What is your favorite snack food? Would you rather try Jam Jerky or Glowing Jelly?
7. Who is the hero you would like to meet?
8. What other books, shows, or movies does this story remind you of?
9. What do you think will happen in the next book in the series?
10. If you could talk to the author, what is one question you would ask her?

For more discussion questions, visit:
scaredybat.com/book3bonus

About the Author

Marina J. Bowman is a writer and explorer who travels the world searching for wildly fantastical stories to share with her readers. Ever since she was a child, she has been fascinated with uncovering long lost secrets and chasing the mythical, magical, and supernatural. For her current story, Marina is investigating a charming town in the northern US, where vampires and humans live in harmony.

Marina enjoys sailing, flying, and nearly all other forms of transportation. She never strays far from the ocean for long, as it brings her both inspiration and peace. She stays away from the spotlight to maintain privacy and ensure the more unpleasant secrets she uncovers don't catch up with her.

As a matter of survival, Marina nearly always communicates with the public through her representative, Devin Cowick. Ms. Cowick is an entrepreneur who shares Marina's passion for travel and creative storytelling and is the co-founder of Code Pineapple.

Marina's last name is pronounced baʊmən, and rhymes with "now then."

Made in the USA
Las Vegas, NV
11 December 2020